Owen Foote, Second Grade
★ STRONGMAN ★

Owen Foote, Second Grade
★ STRONGMAN ★

by Stephanie Greene

Clarion Books/New York

Clarion Books
a Houghton Mifflin Company imprint
215 Park Avenue South, New York, NY 10003
Text copyright © 1996 by Stephanie Greene
Illustrations © 1996 by Dee deRosa

Illustrations executed in pencil
Text is 14/19-point Palatino

For information about this and other Houghton Mifflin trade and
reference books and multimedia products, visit The Bookstore
at Houghton Mifflin on the World Wide Web at
(http://www.hmco.com/trade/).

Printed in the USA.

Library of Congress Cataloging-in-Publication Data

Greene, Stephanie.
Owen Foote, second grade strongman / by Stephanie Greene ;
illustrated by Dee deRosa.
p.   cm.
Summary: Owen, a second grader who is being teased for his
small size, discovers that his friend Joseph is just as concerned
about being overweight, and they share their fear of being
humiliated by the school nurse.
ISBN 0-395-72098-2
[1. Self-esteem—Fiction.   2. School—Fiction.]
I. deRosa, Dee, ill.   II. Title.
PZ7.G84340w   1996
[Fic]—dc20   95-11693
CIP
AC
VB 10 9 8 7 6 5 4 3 2 1

To my mother and father
and Oliver, too

Contents

Owen Foote, Second Grade
★ STRONGMAN ★

★ 1 ★

Lean and Mean

Owen's grandfather was a strongman. A professional strongman.

"What's that mean?" Joseph asked. Joseph was Owen's best friend.

"It was his job," Owen said. "He got paid for being strong."

"Wow," Joseph said. "I'd like a job like that."

They were lying on their stomachs in Owen's bedroom. Joseph was spending the night. They had stripped down to their underwear. They had been looking at their bodies in the mirror on Owen's closet door and making muscles.

Now they were looking at pictures of Owen's grandfather.

"Look at this one," Owen said. "Twelve against one!"

In the picture Owen was holding, his grandfather was playing tug-of-war against twelve sailors. The sailors were holding on to one end of a long chain. Owen's grandfather was at the other end. He was holding the chain between his teeth. He was winning.

"Are you sure this isn't trick photography?" Joseph said.

"No way," said Owen. "He was strong, all right."

One of the other pictures showed Owen's grandfather bending a huge piece of metal. Other pieces of metal were on the ground all around him. They were bent into circles and loops.

In another, he was tearing a quarter in half.

Then there was one of him just standing in a yard like a regular grandfather. He was holding

a little boy in his arms. The boy was Owen's dad. His ears stuck out and he looked happy.

Owen liked this one best. He studied it all the time. He thought if he looked close enough, maybe he could discover his grandfather's secret.

He and Joseph leaned over it now.

"He looks pretty normal," Joseph said. "He doesn't look like he lifts weights or anything."

"He didn't have to," Owen said. "He was born that way." He sat up. This was important. "And his blood is running through my veins."

He held out his arm. They stared at his wrist. It was so small it looked like a chicken's wrist. His veins looked like a chicken's veins.

Owen was small for his age, his mother always said. He hated that expression. She tried to say it very softly so she wouldn't hurt his feelings. But he always heard.

"I want to meet this guy," Joseph said. "Is he alive?"

"I think so," said Owen. "I'm not sure."

"What do you mean, you're not sure?" said Joseph. He sounded amazed. "He's your grandfather, isn't he?" He picked up a small red weight from the floor and started lifting it up and down over his head.

Owen picked up the other weight. "I think I saw him when I was a baby." He started bending his arm up and down.

The weights belonged to Owen's mother. She did exercises with them in front of the television every morning.

When Owen was little she wouldn't let him use them. She said they were dangerous. Now that he was in second grade, she said it was okay.

"Just be careful," she'd warned him. "You can hurt yourself with those things."

He'd thought she must be using them wrong. Then one day he knocked himself on the head with one. Boy, did it hurt.

Owen started doing deep knee bends. Joseph put down his weight and started doing push-ups.

He gave up after two. Joseph was big, but he was soft.

"You're kind of like that boy made out of dough on television," Owen said when Joseph collapsed.

"Thanks a lot," Joseph said.

"You can't help it," Owen said. "You inherited it. I'm an ectomorph and you're an endomorph."

"We sound like lizards," Joseph said. That made Owen laugh. He got down on his hands and knees and started nibbling at Joseph's ankles.

"I'm a what?" Joseph asked as he fell on Owen. He was very ticklish.

"An endomorph," Owen said. "It means you're kind of fattish and oversized."

"Gross," Joseph said.

"I read about it in the encyclopedia," Owen said. "Everyone's born with a certain kind of body. I was born with a skinny, bony one."

There was a knock at the door. Owen's sister, Lydia, put her head around the corner. Lydia was in the sixth grade.

"Dinner's ready." She stared. Owen and Joseph shrieked. Owen dove for his quilt. Joseph ran into the closet and slammed the door. There was a short silence in the room.

"Nice bodies," Lydia said. "You won't find any food in there, Joseph." She shut the bedroom door. They heard her yell, "Hey, Mom!" as she ran down the stairs.

"You could write to your grandfather," Joseph said as they got dressed. "Maybe he could give us a few tips."

"Yeah, maybe he could come visit," Owen said. "I'll have to ask my dad."

They started down the stairs.

"So does this 'endo' person ever get lean and mean?" Joseph said.

"I don't think so," said Owen, "but I think animals like him."

"Great," said Joseph. He made a face.

"Babies, too," Owen said.

"Double great."

★2★

Darn That Old Mrs. Jackson!

On Tuesday at three o'clock, Owen stormed into the house. He slammed the back door. He hurled his backpack onto the counter and threw himself into a chair. He kicked the leg of the kitchen table.

"Owen, what's wrong?" his mother said.

Owen crossed his arms over his chest and glowered.

Lydia had come into the kitchen behind him. "Next Thursday's height-and-weight-chart day," she said. She picked up an apple. "Owen hates it."

"Oh, sweetie," his mother said. She sat down beside him and ruffled his hair. "You'll do just fine."

Ever since Owen could remember, people had been ruffling his hair. It was blond and curly and soft. The girls in kindergarten couldn't keep their hands off it. It made Owen furious.

So on the first day of first grade he decided to put an end to it. When Tara Tilt reached her hand out toward his head, he kicked her. Right on her shin, as hard as he could.

On the first day of first grade he was sent to the principal's office for the first time.

He thought maybe the number one was his unlucky number.

"How would you like it if all the girls ruffled your hair?" he asked Mr. Mahoney. Mr. Mahoney had a flattop. He used to be in the Marines. He still was, on the weekends.

When Owen was in kindergarten he thought Mr. Mahoney looked kind. In first grade, closer up, he looked strict.

"No kicking," Mr. Mahoney said. He was a man of few words.

"No ruffling, no kicking."

"Deal."

Owen could tell he was going to like Mr. Mahoney. He hadn't tried to tell him that someday he'd be glad to have girls admire his hair. That's what Owen's father had said.

"Kids don't care about when they're grown up," Owen had told his dad. "They just care about now."

After that, the only person who dared touch his hair was his mother. And usually Owen didn't mind. But not today. Not even his mother.

He jerked his head away.

"It won't be bad, Owen," his mother said. She sounded sad. "I didn't know you minded so much."

That's because Owen had never told her. Height-and-weight-chart day was the worst day of his life. It was the day all the kids got measured. Right in front of everyone else. So everyone would know how much you'd grown in a year.

Last year Owen was the smallest in his class. He knew he would be this year, too.

"I hate Mrs. Jackson," he said loudly. "She has a big mouth!"

Mrs. Jackson was the school nurse. She'd been the school nurse for twenty-three years. She always said she felt as if the children at Chesterfield School were her own. To Owen, that meant she felt free to yell at them.

"Owen, that's rude," his mother said. "You hardly know Mrs. Jackson. You've only ever been to the nurse's office to be weighed."

"I'd rather die," Owen said. "I'd rather die a slow, painful death from a tarantula bite on the playground than go to the nurse's office. Every time she opens her mouth it's like she's talking over the loudspeaker. She's dumb!"

His mother stood up. "I can see there's no point in pursuing this conversation. Would you like a snack?"

"No."

"No what?"

"No, thank you!" he shouted. He practically jumped out of his chair. "Is Dad home?"

Owen's dad was a teacher at a college. Sometimes he got home from work at lunchtime. Other days he worked all day.

"Not yet," his mother said. "Why don't you go upstairs and relax? I'll send Dad up when he gets home."

"I was going to do that anyway," Owen said.

He stomped up the stairs. Each time he put his foot down he did it as hard as he could. It took longer to get upstairs, but it made him feel better.

He slammed his bedroom door. He fell face down on his bed. Darn that old Mrs. Jackson. She was dumb, dumb, dumb!

He knew next Thursday was going to be awful. It was going to be just as bad as last year. No, worse than last year. This year everyone else would be bigger than ever. He'd look even smaller.

Last year, she had made them all stand in a line. Then, one by one, she'd weighed them and measured them.

"Why, Owen Foote," she said in her loud, booming voice when it was Owen's turn, "you're just a pip-squeak."

Everyone in line laughed. Even the girls.

But especially Ben Carter. Ben was the biggest boy in the class. And the meanest. He had stayed back one year. He was a second grader who knew how to be mean like a third grader.

Being mean to other kids was definitely something you got better at as you got older.

Before height-and-weight-chart day Ben had left Owen alone. He laughed at Owen's jokes. He asked Owen for the answers to a lot of questions.

But after the pip-squeak incident, every time Owen walked past his desk, Ben said, "Squeak, squeak, squeak," like a mouse.

Owen punched his pillow. Fat, old Mrs. Jackson.

There was a knock on his door. His dad put his head around the corner. "Is it safe to come in?"

Owen sat up. "What's your code number?"

"268."

"Okay, you're my father." Last summer Owen had read a science-fiction story about aliens. First the aliens invaded this farm family. Then they put on masks and tricked the kids into thinking that they were really their parents. When the kids hugged them good night the aliens paralyzed them and dissected their brains.

Right after that, Owen gave everyone in his family a secret number. Kind of like a password. Just in case it could happen in real life. He wanted his brains all in one piece.

His dad sat down on the end of the bed. "Mom said you wanted to see me."

"Can I write to your father?" Owen asked.

"He's dead, Owen. He died when you were a baby."

"Oh." Owen thought for a minute. "I think I remember him."

His dad smiled. "We took you to see him just before he died. You were only a month old. But who knows, maybe you do remember him. Why do you want to write to him?"

"I want to know when he started getting so strong," Owen said. "I mean, was he a shrimp one day and then strong the next?"

"The way I always heard it, he bit through a spoon when he was eight," his dad said. "That's when the strength started."

"Wow," Owen said. "With his bare teeth?"

"Apparently," said Dad. "He was sitting at the breakfast table and picked up a spoon and bit it into two pieces."

"Cool," Owen breathed.

"Tell you what," his dad said. "Why don't you write to Gran? She'd love to tell you about him. She knows all the stories. They were married for almost fifty years."

"Great idea." Owen was feeling better already. He told his dad about height-and-weight-chart day. About Mrs. Jackson's voice and how it carried. About how she called him a pip-squeak in front of the whole class.

"Mrs. Jackson doesn't sound like a particularly tactful woman," his dad said. "She really put you on the spot."

"You can say that again," Owen said. His dad was pretty smart. "Were you ever at the bottom of the chart?"

"Sure," said his dad. "I didn't get a growth spurt until I was fourteen."

Owen groaned.

"You may not be exactly like me," his father said. "Remember the food pyramid."

Owen loved the food pyramid. He loved the way the little pictures showed which foods you should eat a lot of and which foods you should avoid. He'd drawn one himself. It had a tiny fish and little loaves of bread. His favorite drawing was a miniature cluster of purple grapes.

His mother had hung it on the refrigerator. It was still there.

"Keep eating your vegetables and carbohydrates and protein," his father went on. "Get a lot of exercise. You may be big and strong long before you're fourteen."

"I don't need big and strong right away. I just want tall by next Thursday."

His dad laughed. "Let's go check out the garden."

Owen followed Dad down the stairs, three at a time. He'd write his letter tonight.

He could ask Gran if his grandfather was small to start with. He could ask if he was ever the smallest in his class.

Maybe she could even tell him what signs to look for that his own strength was starting. As far as he was concerned, it couldn't start a minute too soon.

He could hardly wait to hear from Gran.

★ 3 ★

Pudgie-Wudgie

It was Saturday. Owen was doing what he liked to do most on Saturday mornings, working on a new invention. Today it was a silent alarm clock.

He'd read about a man who made one using sixty corks. He loved that idea, sixty corks going bonk!bonk!bonk! gently on someone's head. He thought it would be a nice way to wake up.

Not that he needed help. He woke up with the birds. But Lydia had a terrible time waking up. He decided to test his invention out on her. She'd love it.

He went down to the kitchen. There were only six corks in the drawer. Then he saw his basketball in the corner.

He carried it back upstairs and put it in a pillowcase. He tied one end of a rope around the pillowcase and the other end around a stick. Then he went into Lydia's room and wedged the stick behind her headboard.

Just as he was standing back, trying to figure out how to get the alarm to trigger at the right time, Lydia walked in.

"What are you doing in here?" Without waiting for an answer, she grabbed a book and jumped on her bed. The headboard jiggled, the stick loosened, and the basketball hit her squarely on the head.

Lydia shrieked. She grabbed her head with both hands.

Owen was thrilled. "It works!" he shouted.

Lydia jumped up from her bed. "Mom, Owen

tried to kill me!" She started punching him on the shoulder. He started karate-kicking in self-defense.

"That's the last time I waste a great idea on you!" he shouted. He kicked her shin.

"What's going on?"

Their mother was standing in the doorway. She had a mop in one hand, a duster in the other. Owen suddenly remembered his parents were having people over for dinner. And that meant his mother was already in a bad mood.

Whenever they had guests, his mother spent the whole day cleaning the house. She made his father help. It put them both in a terrible mood. They got mad at Owen and Lydia for the tiniest thing.

"I think I have a concussion," Lydia whined. "Owen dropped a rock on my head."

"It was a basketball," he muttered into his chest. He didn't dare look his mother in the eye.

Mrs. Foote held out the mop to Lydia. "After you mop the living room, you can polish the silver." She looked at Owen. "You go prune the lilac bush next to the garage."

That's how they always got punished in their house. They had to do some work. Owen was happy to get outside work. His father had taught him how to prune. He loved it. It didn't even feel like work.

But he didn't tell his mother that.

"Darn," he said. He skinned out, fast.

"No fair," he heard Lydia say. "Owen loves to prune."

Owen whipped into the kitchen. He karate-kicked at the refrigerator door. Then he saw the cake on the counter. It was his mother's world-famous chocolate cake. She served it at practically every dinner party. It was always a hit.

She never told anyone it had sauerkraut in it until after they'd eaten it.

The first time she made it, she tried it out on the family. She told them about the sauerkraut right after Owen put his first bite in his mouth.

He practically choked to death.

After that she decided she should wait until people were finished eating.

He went over and stood by the cake. The smell of chocolate filled the air. He looked back over his shoulder. Then he ran his finger along the bottom edge of the cake. It was the perfect spot, where the frosting dripped down the sides and made a pool on the plate.

If he was careful, he could run his finger around the whole cake and no one would ever know.

"How many times have I told you?"

Owen spun around, his finger in his mouth.

"The next time you want to test out an invention, do it on yourself." His mother opened the closet door. She took out a dustpan. "And don't lay a finger on that cake, do you hear me?"

Owen nodded his head up and down. "Sure, Mom." He edged his way toward the back door, keeping his back to the counter and his eyes on his mother. When his hand felt the doorknob, he turned and bolted into the garage.

He grabbed the pruners and went outside. First he cut a few branches, then stood back to look. Cut a few more, took another look. Like an artist inspecting his masterpiece.

"Want to spend the night at my house?" Joseph was standing in the driveway. He was holding his violin case. "My mother said I could stop on the way to my lesson and invite you."

"Owen's being punished, Joseph," a voice called.

Joseph jumped. He looked around.

Mrs. Foote stuck her head out of an upstairs window.

"He can't talk right now, Joseph. He's trying to learn how to act like a civilized person by communing with nature."

"My mother said, could Owen spend the night," Joseph said. He sounded as if he was ready to run at a moment's notice. Owen knew that Joseph probably wasn't sure what Mrs. Foote was talking about. But he sure understood her tone of voice.

"That would be wonderful," she said. "He'll come over as soon as he's finished a few chores. Unless, of course, I see one more fingerprint in my icing, in which case he'll be spending the next thousand years in his room."

Owen rolled his eyes. Joseph backed down the driveway, holding his violin case in front of him like a shield. "See you later," he whispered.

"Your mother's scary."

It was nine o'clock. They were lying on the floor in Joseph's bedroom. They were in their sleeping bags. Mrs. Hobbs had said they could read for half an hour.

"Not when you live with her," Owen said. "You get used to her. You just can't say anything you don't want her to hear. She has ears like a bat."

Joseph already knew that from last year. They had been playing in Owen's playroom when

Joseph's stomach rumbled. "Ask your mother if we can have a snack," he had whispered to Owen.

"Not now, Joseph," Mrs. Foote had called from the kitchen. "It's too close to dinner."

"Maybe we should learn sign language," he said to Owen now.

"It won't help, her eyesight's good, too," Owen said.

Owen took a book from the shelf above his head. He opened the cover. On the first page someone had written: "To Pudgie-Wudgie from Donna."

"Who's Pudgie-Wudgie?" he said.

"Me."

"You?" Owen looked over at Joseph. Joseph's face was pink. "Who calls you that?"

"My cousin in Vermont. I hate her."

Owen didn't even know Joseph had a cousin. "I didn't know you were called that."

"I'm not. She just says it to make me mad."

"Why don't you punch her, or something?"

"I did. She gave me a bloody nose."

"Why don't you tell your mother?"

"I did. She says I should ignore it. If I don't get mad, she says, Donna will stop."

Owen didn't think anyone could be called Pudgie-Wudgie and ignore it. Not even a grownup.

Parents always said things like that. They said names could never hurt you. But kids were smarter. They knew they could.

"You're not pudgy," Owen told Joseph. He thought Joseph's size was great. Much better than his own.

"Yes, I am," Joseph said. "You think being big is so great. But some people aren't just big, they're fat. Being fat is a pain in the neck."

Owen was amazed. He'd never known Joseph felt like that. Joseph was his best friend. Owen thought he knew everything there was to know about Joseph.

"Remember that time in kindergarten?" Joseph said. "When I got sick all over Mrs. Nichols?"

Owen remembered, all right. One day the boy sitting next to Joseph had reached over and punched him in the stomach. For no reason at all. When Mrs. Nichols came over to help, Joseph coughed a few small coughs and threw up. It went all over her shoes.

"You threw up because Henry punched you in the stomach." Owen said.

"It wasn't that. That didn't even hurt. I was nervous because Mrs. Nichols wanted me to lift up my shirt to see if there was a bruise or anything."

"So?"

"So I didn't want everyone to see my fat stomach."

Mrs. Hobbs yelled up from downstairs. "Lights out, boys."

Joseph got up and turned off the light. He crawled back into his sleeping bag.

There was silence in the room. Then Joseph's voice came through the dark. "I don't mind so much anymore. I think my stomach's getting smaller. It'll probably stretch out as I get taller, too. And I'm hoping your grandfather can give me a few tips."

"I forgot to tell you. He can't come. He's dead."

"Darn it." Owen could hear Joseph thinking. Finally he said, "At least you don't have to worry. You got his blood."

"Yeah," Owen agreed. He thought about that. Then he had an idea. He sat up. "Maybe we could do a transfusion."

But Joseph was already asleep. Owen could tell—his breathing was slow and even. Joseph always fell asleep like that. In a second.

But not Owen. He lay down and kept on thinking.

He thought maybe Joseph was right about his stomach stretching out. It did look a little smaller than last year, now that he thought about it.

But he knew Joseph was wrong about size. He knew it was better to be big. Even fat.

Anything but small. Being small was practically the worst thing that could happen to you.

Unless you were small, you couldn't understand. And it wasn't something he could
explain. Not even to his best friend.

★ 4 ★

Human Pretzels for Dinner

Owen was about to miss the first bell. It was the same way every morning. Every morning he walked to school and made it just seconds before the bell.

"You were almost late," Joseph always said.

"I was just in time," Owen always insisted.

Now he could see Joseph waiting for him on the playground. He was leaning against the fence. He had his watch up in front of his face. Owen knew he was watching the second hand go around and around and worrying.

Owen felt like an Olympic runner heading for the finish line. He knew Joseph hated being late. He knew Joseph rode the bus just so he would be on time. But then he always ruined it by waiting for him, Owen, so they could go in together.

And Owen didn't care about being on time. He liked to walk.

"You can listen to the birds," he told Joseph. "You can find amazing things."

And Owen did find amazing things. Birds with broken wings. Fire-bellied salamanders. Quarters.

One time he even found a huge bone he was sure was a fossilized dinosaur thighbone.

"Hey, Joseph!" he yelled now. "Look what I found."

He held out his backpack very carefully. Joseph peered inside.

There was a box turtle. It had a high-domed shell with yellow triangles on it. Its head and legs were tucked in tight.

"Isn't he great?" Owen said.

"I don't know," Joseph said. "I can't see very much of him. Come on, Owen, we're late."

"He has some kind of tumor on his neck." They joined the sea of children flowing into the school. "I might have to operate."

Joseph stopped dead in his tracks. The kid behind him bumped into him. "Move it or lose it," she said.

"What do you mean, operate? You're not a doctor." Joseph's face was white.

"I have a Swiss Army knife, don't I?" Owen said. "There are books, right? I can read, can't I?"

"You can't just operate because you read it in a book," Joseph said hotly. "You're going to make me a nervous wreck, you know that?"

Owen's motto was: "If you don't know it, look it up." It was partly because his mother worked in a library. But it was mainly because that's the way he was.

He'd always been like that. Just the way Joseph had always been a worrier. When they graduated from kindergarten, Owen won the "Little Professor" award. Joseph won the "Good Kid" award.

They were best friends from the first day. Owen knew Joseph would always back him up, no matter how nervous it made him.

Owen put his pack into his cubbyhole. He propped it open with his ruler. "He needs air," he whispered as they sat down.

Ben walked past Owen's desk. "Hey, Owen, bend any metal bars lately?" He flipped Owen's notebook onto the floor.

Owen glared at Joseph. He must have blabbed all over the playground.

"I couldn't help it," Joseph told him. "You were late. I had to talk about something."

"Great, really great." Owen knew Joseph had told everyone about his grandfather. They would all give Owen a hard time.

If you have a professional strongman for a grandfather and you're big, it's one thing. If you're a shrimp, it's another.

Mrs. LeDuc called for their attention. It was time for science. They had been learning about electricity. Today they were going to start a new project.

First, each of them was going to build a box with a secret latch. Then they were going to put a small alarm in it. If anyone opened the box without permission, the alarm would go off.

Everyone was excited. They all imagined what they would put into their boxes. How great it would be to trap their sneaky brothers and sisters. Even their parents! Owen got so involved in his box he forgot everything else.

At lunchtime, Joseph slid into the seat next to Owen in the cafeteria. "Sorry," Joseph said. He sat there without opening his lunch box.

"About what?" Owen said. He bit into his sandwich. "I can hardly wait to trap Lydia. Maybe I'll put a spider in my box. I can terrify her and get her into trouble at the same time."

"Sorry I told about your grandfather." Joseph looked miserable. "I didn't say he was dead, though."

"Good," Owen said. "If anyone bugs me I'll pretend he's coming for a visit."

"Yeah, invite them over for a barbecue," Joseph said. "Tell them you're having human pretzels for dinner."

They laughed. Owen choked on his milk and spit some out. That made them laugh even harder. Joseph opened his lunch box and started eating.

"Think you can tear this dollar bill in half, strongman?" Ben said in a loud voice. He was standing behind Owen. He waved the money in Owen's face.

"Sure." Owen grabbed it out of Ben's hand. He held it up to his lips and pulled down quickly on one side. There was a loud tearing noise.

Everyone at the table stopped eating. "Better close your mouth, Ben," Owen said. "You're catching flies."

He held up the dollar bill. It was in one piece.

"How'd you do that?" Anthony Petrocelli said. "It sounded so real."

"You're a riot." Ben grabbed the dollar bill and stomped off.

"You just blow on the edge while you pretend to tear it," Owen said. "It sounds like it's really tearing."

Everyone started practicing on their napkins.

"I think you're going to be even stronger than your grandfather," Joseph said.

"How come?" said Owen.

"All he could tear in half was quarters," Joseph joked. "You're already tearing dollars."

"Yeah," said Owen. He beat his fists on his chest like a gorilla. "Me want hundred-dollar bills!"

This time it was Joseph who spit out his milk.

★ 5 ★

Mayday, Mayday

It was Thursday and there was nothing any-one could do about it. Owen didn't even have the heart to operate on his turtle. He left it in a box in his bedroom.

Owen didn't feel like eating breakfast, either. He ate anyway. When he didn't eat, his parents got upset. And he could already tell his mother was worried about height-and-weight-chart day. He figured she was probably going to give him a pep talk.

He was right. When he was putting on his

backpack, she leaned over and said, "Look me right in the eye, Owen. I want to make sure you're in there."

That's what she said when she wanted to make sure he was listening. It worked, too. It was hard to ignore her when they were eyeball-to-eyeball.

"I don't want you to get upset about this height-and-weight business," she said. "You are who you are. Save your energy for the things you can change."

It was the kind of thing she always said. At least she had stopped telling him it didn't matter whether he was big or small. But the idea of saving his energy appealed to him. He knew it made sense.

"Okay, Mom," he said.

She kissed him. "You're a wonderful boy and I love you very much."

"Don't start getting all mushy." He pulled out of her grasp and wiped his cheek with his sleeve.

Sometimes it felt good to sit in her lap with her arms around him and her chin resting on his head.

But other times, when he was in a bad mood, having her near him made his eyes water. Like now.

"Promise me one thing," she said as he opened the door. "Don't lose your temper with Mrs. Jackson. I want you to be polite, no matter what."

"No way," Owen said. "I'm not making promises I can't keep."

That ought to stop her, he thought. That's what she always says to me. He shut the door before she could say anything else.

"Mayday, mayday," Joseph called. He was waiting at the end of the driveway.

"What are you doing here?" Owen said. Joseph never walked to school. Owen thought it would probably take a major disaster to make Joseph walk.

He suddenly realized Joseph hated height-and-weight-chart day, too.

"I thought maybe I could lose a few pounds before I get to school," Joseph said. He didn't sound too hopeful.

"How come?"

"So Mrs. Jackson won't poke me in the stomach again and tell me I'm watching too much television."

"You don't have a television," Owen said.

"I know that."

"Is that what she said last year?"

"Yep."

They turned the corner. Owen kicked a stone. It rolled off into the gutter. "Grownups always think they're the boss."

"Yeah," Joseph said. "I guess that's because they are."

They walked the rest of the way without talking. They didn't find a single wonderful thing.

At ten o'clock, Mrs. LeDuc clapped her hands. "Okay, class. Finish what you're doing and line up. We're going to Mrs. Jackson's office."

She had to tell them two times to hurry. There

was a lot of pushing and shoving. So many kids got sent to the back of the line that it started to look like the front.

Finally, they were ready. They walked down the hall to Mrs. Jackson's door. She was waiting.

"Hello, children," she boomed. They filed into her office. No one dared shove. She might pick them to go first. They'd be in trouble before they even stepped on the scale.

"I'm going to take you in alphabetical order," she said. "Nancy Barron, you're first, dear."

Nancy was the only one who didn't mind being first. She actually loved being first. Ever since kindergarten she had bragged about being in the fiftieth percentile. That was how doctors measured. It meant she was right in the middle. Not too tall, not too short. Not too fat, not too thin.

"Perfect," Mrs. Jackson said. "You're just the right height and weight." Nancy beamed.

Mrs. Jackson went down the alphabet. Since Joseph's last name was Hobbs, Owen was before him. But Ben was before Owen.

"Ben Carter," Mrs. Jackson said.

Ben stepped forward. Mrs. Jackson frowned. He stepped onto the scale.

"Looks like someone has been eating too many potato chips," she said. "If you're not careful, Ben, you're going to grow up to be fat."

Ben turned red. Owen had never seen him turn red before. Usually Ben made everyone else turn red.

But it didn't make Owen feel good. It made him feel embarrassed. He couldn't believe it. He actually felt sorry for Ben Carter.

Mrs. Jackson measured a few more kids. Then it was Owen's turn. He walked right up to the scale. He didn't have time to feel worried. He was still feeling bad for Ben.

"Well, Owen," Mrs. Jackson said as she moved the weights around, "you're looking good this year." She peered closely at the number. "Forty-five pounds."

She guided him over to the height chart on the wall. She peered again. Then she patted his head.

"You're headed in the right direction," she said. "Keep up the good work."

It was over. Owen walked to the end of the line. He couldn't believe it. She hadn't called him a pip-squeak. She'd said he was headed in the right direction!

He felt as if he'd just come out of the woods after being lost for ten days and nights. He felt relieved. He felt great.

Then he heard two small coughs.

"Joseph Hobbs, whatever am I going to do with you?" Owen looked up. Joseph was on the scale.

"You have simply got to start getting some exercise," Mrs. Jackson said. She tapped her finger on his stomach. "Too much television."

Joseph gave another small cough.

Owen knew those coughs. He knew Joseph would die if he threw up now. It would go all over the scale. Maybe all over Mrs. Jackson. A too-fat kid with throw-up all over him would be a hard image to live down. Kids would never let Joseph forget it.

"Mrs. Jackson, don't you think you should keep your voice down a little?" someone said.

Every head turned to look at Owen. He couldn't believe it. It was his voice they'd heard. He, Owen, had just opened his big mouth.

"Excuse me, Owen?" Mrs. Jackson said. Her voice was like ice.

"It's your voice," Owen said. There was a ringing in his ears. He felt like throwing up himself. "First you make Ben feel bad, now Joseph. I just think you shouldn't talk so loud, that's all."

Mrs. Jackson was standing over him. Her face looked like it was carved out of rock. "We do not speak to adults like that in Chesterfield School," she said. She pronounced every word clearly. Just the way his mother did sometimes. It meant only one thing.

"You go right down to Mr. Mahoney's office, young man," she said. "I'm sure he'll have something to say about this."

Owen walked out of the room. "Let this be a lesson to you all," he heard her say. Then the door swung closed behind him.

★ **6** ★

"Way To Go, Kid"

Mr. Mahoney was waiting for him. He already knew the whole story. Kids said he always seemed to know the story by the time you got to his office.

Owen didn't know how he did it. He wondered if Mr. Mahoney had a transistor radio in his ear. Like a Secret Service guy. That way, the teachers could send messages to him all day long.

Owen was dying to get a closer look at Mr. Mahoney's ears. But he didn't think now was the right time.

"I am not happy seeing you here like this, Owen," Mr. Mahoney said.

"Me neither," said Owen.

"When you are in this school, you are to treat adults with respect," Mr. Mahoney said. "That means no talking back, no wisecracks. When a teacher tells you to do something, you do it. Do you understand?"

Owen knew Mr. Mahoney didn't really want his opinion. He knew he really just wanted a simple "yes."

"What about Mrs. Jackson?" he said. "She doesn't treat us with respect. She makes kids feel bad. She tells them they're fat, and that they eat too much, and she has this loud voice that carries all over the whole school."

Mr. Mahoney knew about Mrs. Jackson's voice. All the teachers did. Sometimes they ducked into the bathroom when they heard her coming. Once, Mr. Mahoney had ducked into the art closet.

"Mrs. Jackson doesn't mean to hurt anyone's feelings," he said. "She's just doing her job. If you have a problem with something she says, you can talk to her privately."

"I couldn't help it," Owen said. "It just came out."

"That's why we teach self-control," said Mr. Mahoney. "No one can say exactly what they want to say exactly when they want to say it. Not even the commander of the United States Marine Corps."

Owen couldn't believe it. That was exactly what his mother always said to him. Except she said, "Not even the President of the United States."

Owen wondered if there was some kind of manual they all read. "How To Be a Grownup," or something like that. If there was, he was going to rewrite it when he grew up. It had a lot of mistakes.

"I do not want to see you in here again for the same reason." Mr. Mahoney was almost through, Owen could tell. He had picked up a pencil. "Do you understand?"

"Yes," Owen said.

"And I want you to stop back in here on your way home," Mr. Mahoney said. "I think your parents will want to hear about this."

Oh, they'll love hearing about this, Owen thought.

When he came out of the office, Lydia was standing outside. Some kids from his class were standing behind her.

"I can't believe you, Owen," Lydia said. "I can't believe you insulted Mrs. Jackson right to her face."

Owen's heart sank. If Lydia thought it was bad, it was really bad.

"Way to go, kid." Someone slapped him on the back. It practically knocked him over. "Sticking up for your fellow man."

It was Clyde Barnes, a seventh grader. He was definitely cool. He was a computer genius. He was captain of the soccer team. He had a streak of purple hair and he wore an earring.

If Clyde Barnes slapped you on the back, it

meant good things. Especially if you were only in the second grade.

"What happened? What happened?" Everyone was crowding around Owen.

He looked over his shoulder at the office door. "You want to get me killed?" he whispered. "Let's get out of here."

"If Mr. Mahoney didn't kill you, Mom and Dad will," Lydia called after him.

Owen didn't care. He'd been slapped on the back by Clyde Barnes. If he had to die, he'd do it like a man.

★ 7 ★

Boys Are Daring People

Owen was in the doghouse.

That meant everyone in his family was mad at him.

His mother and father were mad because he'd been rude to Mrs. Jackson. Lydia was mad because when her parents got mad at Owen about his manners, they got mad at her, too.

"You children have got to learn," their father said at breakfast. "Manners are going to matter your entire life. Whether you like it or not, that's how people judge you."

"I didn't do anything," Lydia complained. "Just because Owen's a slob doesn't mean I am, too." She took her lunch bag and left the room.

Owen kept eating. It was his most-hated cereal —oatmeal. Lumps and slime, he called it.

He knew he couldn't make one false move. He could feel his mother waiting, ready to pounce. She still had some anger left in her.

Last night both she and Dad had yelled at him. They got madder about bad manners than practically anything else, Owen thought. If Mr. Mahoney's letter had said he'd bopped some kid on the nose, they wouldn't have gotten nearly as mad.

But about manners, forget it. Self-control was right up there, too. They said this time he'd forgotten both. This time he was in double trouble.

"I'm proud of you for sticking up for Joseph," his father had said when he came up to say good night. "But you should have done it a different way."

Owen was reading in bed. "You had to be there, Dad," he said, shaking his head. "Joseph was seconds away from throw-up city."

"Maybe so, but I think you owe Mrs. Jackson an apology."

"No way!" Owen had thrown down his book. "I didn't do anything wrong!"

"I can't make you do it, Owen. It's your decision." His father stood up to leave. "But I don't think the air will be cleared until you tell her you're sorry."

I'll live in a smog, then, Owen had thought. At least I won't be able to see her.

This morning the oatmeal was slimier than usual. He bet his mother had planned it that way.

"I want you to come straight home after school," she was saying. "I have some grocery shopping to do. I want you with me."

Today was Friday. She knew he always played soccer after school on Friday. She knew he hated grocery shopping.

He didn't say a word.

★

Joseph ran up to him as he rounded the corner to school.

"Did you get in trouble?" he panted. He looked worried.

"Kind of," Owen said. He didn't want to make Joseph feel any worse. Knowing Joseph, he probably hadn't slept all night.

They walked across the playground. "At least you did okay," Joseph said. "My mother said I have to go on a diet."

"Just follow the food pyramid," Owen said. "You can't go wrong."

"Yeah," Joseph said glumly, "but all the good stuff's at the top and I can never remember the stuff at the bottom."

"I'll draw you one," Owen said. "You can put it on your refrigerator."

"Thanks," Joseph said. He didn't sound hopeful.

Fridays at school were easy. First the second graders had art class. Then they had gym. By lunchtime, they could see the light at the end of the tunnel. Saturday was straight ahead.

At lunchtime Owen had to walk past Mrs. Jackson's office. He tucked his chin to his chest and kept his head down. He walked as fast as he could without running. His heart was pounding so hard he thought he could see his shirt move up and down.

When he got to the cafeteria, everyone pushed and shoved to sit next to him. They all wanted to know what his parents had said. What his punishment was.

"I have to go grocery shopping after school," he told them.

"Gross," said Anthony Petrocelli.

"That's not so bad," Michael Ross said. "Just throw a lot of junk food in the cart when your mother's not looking."

"Yeah, and offer to push the cart. Your mother will think you're just being nice." Ben slid into the spot next to him. "But that way, you can make sure you get into a check-out line with candy."

They all laughed.

"That was pretty cool, what you did," Ben said. "Standing up to old Boom Box."

"Thanks," Owen said. He picked up a fork. "Want to see a great trick?"

He'd been planning on pulling this trick on Ben for a week. Until today, he hadn't planned on telling him it was a trick.

He held the fork in both hands so that the teeth were pointing down. He let them rest gently on the table. His hands covered the handle. Then, groaning as if it was real hard to do, he slowly bent his hands over. It looked as if he was bending the fork in half. As if it was about to break.

"Owen Foote, what are you doing?" It was Mrs. Furlone, the cafeteria monitor. "Is that a school fork?"

Owen held it out. It was straight as an arrow.

"It's just a trick, Mrs. Furlone," he said quickly. He wasn't ready to see Mr. Mahoney again so soon. He felt pretty sure Mr. Mahoney felt the same way. "My father taught it to me."

"Cool," Ben said. He sounded impressed.

"Do it again," Anthony pleaded. They were all shoving each other aside, trying to get a better look.

"Not with a school fork," Mrs. Furlone said. She looked around the table. "You boys are too much, you know that?"

"Boys are daring people," Joseph said happily.

"That's one way of putting it, Joseph," she said. "Leave the fork here when you go, Owen."

Ben rushed up to him after school. "I got this from James LaBonte." He held up a fork. "Show me how you did that."

Owen shook his head. "Monday."

He was going straight home. He knew that if he acted real polite and helped in the grocery store, his mother wouldn't be mad at him anymore.

His mother wasn't the problem.

Mrs. Jackson was.

He'd realized today that her office stood between him and everything he loved most about school. The cafeteria. The gym. The play-ground.

That meant he'd have to walk by a mad Mrs. Jackson about a thousand times a day. He'd have to feel her glaring eyes burning holes into his rude back every day.

Unless he was willing to give up eating and recess, Owen knew he'd have to think of something else. Because even if his feet could carry him, his heart would never make it.

★ 8 ★

Well Worth Waiting For

"Mrs. Jackson."

Owen stood in the doorway. It was bright and early on Monday morning. He had absolutely no idea what he was going to say. But he knew if he was going to say something, it had to be today.

So here he was. And there was Mrs. Jackson. Sitting at her desk, writing. She didn't turn around.

"Mrs. Jackson," he said in a louder voice.

Mrs. Jackson turned and saw him. "Why, Owen, you're just the boy I wanted to see."

She stood up, came over to him, and took him by the arm. "Sit down, dear. I want to talk to you."

Owen thought he must be in a trance. He couldn't speak. His feet shuffled forward as though they had their own brains.

Mrs. Jackson even looked strange. Not like she normally did. Today she looked as if she could be his own grandmother. She was wearing a light blue sweater that matched her eyes. Her eyes had tiny little crinkles all around them. And they were smiling. At him.

Mrs. Jackson was smiling at him as though she was actually glad to see him.

She led him to a chair. He sat down. Then she sat down. She leaned forward. "Owen," she said, "I need to know something, and I think maybe you're the right person to tell me."

Owen couldn't take his eyes off her face.

"Do I talk too loud?" she asked.

Owen blinked. He wasn't in a trance anymore.

He tried not to panic. He knew he should take his time and think before blurting out an answer.

"Actually, you kind of shout," he said finally.

Mrs. Jackson smiled. "Do I hurt people's feelings?"

Owen decided he'd take a trance over this any day. He looked down at his lap. "Sort of."

Mrs. Jackson leaned back in her chair. "Well, then, Teddy was right."

"Who's Teddy?"

"He's my son. He came home from college for the weekend. He's been telling me for years I need a hearing aid. But he says lately I've gotten a lot worse."

She smiled as if Teddy had given her a compliment instead of an insult. "Last night he told me I'd been shouting at him all weekend. He said I'd heard only about half the things he said."

She patted Owen's knee. "That's when I told him all about you and what you said last week."

Owen scrunched down in his chair. He didn't like the way this was going.

"Do you know what he said?"

Owen shook his head. He didn't even want to imagine.

"He said, 'Mom, that kid's got guts.'" She paused. "I think he was right."

Owen sat up straight. He could feel his face burning right up to the tips of his ears. He felt embarrassed and proud at the same time.

"I certainly never wanted to hurt anyone's feelings," Mrs. Jackson said. "And it's not going to happen anymore.

"I've known for years I needed a hearing aid. I just didn't want to admit it. And look at me, I'm a nurse!" She slapped her chest with her hand. "Sometimes it's hard to accept your limitations, no matter who you are."

Owen knew exactly what she meant. "It's like me and my size."

Mrs. Jackson smiled. "That'll change, Owen. You're a late bloomer, that's all."

"What's a late bloomer?"

"Someone who develops a little later than other people—their size or personality or some special talent. Getting their growth late is hard on boys because they're so physical."

"You're telling me," Owen said glumly.

Mrs. Jackson laughed. "You'll get there, Owen. All in good time. Now, I'd better call my doctor. I promised Teddy I'd do it today."

The bell rang. Almost immediately the hall was filled with children. They were shouting and laughing. All Owen wanted was to be out there with them.

"You'd better go," Mrs. Jackson said. "What did you come in here for, by the way? Are you feeling all right?"

"I was going to say I was sorry," said Owen.

"Well, so am I," Mrs. Jackson said. "So now we're even."

Owen walked down the hall. His head was swimming with all the things he had to think about.

Like the fact that Mrs. Jackson couldn't hear. So she never knew she was shouting. That she had a son. That the son said he, Owen, had guts.

But best of all, that he wasn't really a small person. He was a normal person who was a late bloomer. Just like the Better Boy tomatoes his dad had planted last year. They came up way after all the other tomatoes. But when they did, they were beautiful—big, red, and juicy.

His dad had said they were well worth waiting for. And suddenly Owen knew that was the way he was going to grow, too. And that even though the waiting might be tough, it would be well worth waiting for, too.

★9★

What Do You Mean, Nothing?

"Hi, Mom. Mrs. Jackson's getting a hearing aid. What's for snack?"

Owen put his pack on the counter. He lifted the hat off the clown-face cookie jar and peered inside. Lydia came in behind him and shut the door.

"She is?" Mrs. Foote looked up from her newspaper. "How did you find that out?"

Owen took a handful of cookies. "She told me when I went to her office to apologize."

Lydia's mouth fell open. "You, apologize? No way."

"Owen, what do you mean?" his mom said. She sounded surprised. "Stand still and tell me what happened."

"She apologized to me," Owen said.

"No way," Lydia said, louder this time.

"Lydia, will you please stop saying that!" their mom said. She fixed her best stare on Owen. Sometimes it helped pin him down. "Exactly what happened?"

Owen gave a groan. He didn't want to be pinned down. Not right now. He was too full of energy. But he knew his mother wouldn't let him go until she got an explanation. He tried to talk slowly so she would understand.

"Mrs. Jackson said Teddy was home from college and she couldn't hear a word he said so he told her to get a hearing aid and she told him about me, and then she said I'm like a Better Boy tomato."

There, he thought, that ought to do it. He turned to Lydia. "And Teddy says I have guts and he should know, so there."

His mom looked blank. "Mrs. Jackson said you're like a tomato?" she said.

"At least she didn't call him a turkey," said Lydia, "although I don't think a tomato's too good, either."

Owen slumped into a chair. This was going to be harder than he thought. His mother and Lydia were acting as if they couldn't understand plain old English.

He looked at the pile of mail in front of him. The envelope on top had his name on it.

"It's my letter from Gran!" Owen grabbed the envelope and jumped to his feet. "I've got to call Joseph!"

"Wait a minute," his mother said in a warning tone of voice. "We're not through with this."

Owen clasped his hands together and gave her his most pleading face. "Please, Mom, please? It's important."

She looked at him for a long moment. Then he saw her eyes go soft. "All right, but come right back here when you're through."

"You're the best mom in the world!" he shouted. He ran into the study and shut the door.

His grandmother's handwriting was hard to read. It was very small and squiggly. He read the letter once, carefully. Then he picked up the phone and dialed. He read the letter again while he listened to the phone ringing at Joseph's house.

"Hello, Joseph Hobbs speaking."

"It's me. I got a letter from my grandmother."

"Cool. What's it say?"

"Nothing."

"What do you mean, nothing? A letter can't say nothing."

"It doesn't say one single thing about why my grandfather was so strong."

"Oh." At Joseph's end the phone was silent. "What does it say?"

"It says he was a wonderful man who always gave her flowers on her birthday."

"That's all?"

"No. It says he always wore a clean shirt and

tie, even on the weekends." Owen turned the letter over. "Then there's this: 'One time he walked two miles back to a store in a snowstorm to return forty cents extra change they had given him.'"

"That was nice of him."

"She says he ruined his shoes."

Joseph didn't say anything. Owen knew he was probably worrying about his grandfather's shoes.

"Nothing about strength or muscles?" Joseph asked after a moment.

"Nothing. Except at the end." Owen held the letter close to his face. "She says, 'His greatest strength was in his character.' And that's it."

Dead silence. Finally, Joseph said, "What does that mean?"

"I'm not sure. I think it means he had a strong personality, too," Owen said. "Lots of people admire strong personalities."

"I don't know," Joseph said doubtfully, "my mother would kill me if I ruined a pair of shoes."

"Yeah, but not if you were being real honest or something," Owen said.

"I guess." Joseph didn't sound convinced. "Do you think this means the weights won't do any good?"

"Are you kidding?" said Owen. "It means we have to work harder than ever. You'd better get over here."

"I'll be right there," Joseph said.

Owen put down the phone.

The first thing he had to do was look up "character" in the dictionary just to make sure.

Then he thought he'd better start lifting a few weights. He couldn't even wait for Joseph. If he was going to be anything like his grandfather, Owen realized, he was going to have to do it on his own.

How to Perform the "Bending Fork" Trick

1. Hold the fork in your right hand. Your four fingers should cover the handle and your thumb should rest on the top edge (not wrap around the back as it would in a normal grasp).

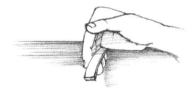

2. Rest the teeth of the fork lightly on the table. Practice "pivoting" the fork by letting go of the top end with your thumb while pushing down against the handle with the side of your hand until the handle almost touches the table.

3. Next, put your left hand over your right hand with the left thumb on top of the right one. You should not be able to see the top end of the fork. Clasp your hands together tightly so it looks as if you have a firm grasp on the fork with both hands.

4. Place the teeth of the fork on the table so that the handle slants toward your body. You are now ready to perform the trick!

5. First, to distract your audience, talk a little bit about how hard this trick is to do and how you're not sure you're strong enough, etc. Then, with a sudden motion, bear down on the fork and let the handle pivot out from under your right hand so that it moves down toward the table. Your clasped hands should cover it up. DO NOT BEND THE FORK! Give a grunt and make a face to show how much effort it's taking.

6. As soon as the fork is "bent," quickly open your hands, grasp the end of the fork with your right-hand fingers and the tines with your left-hand fingers, and pretend you quickly "stretched" it back to straighten it out.

About the Author

Stephanie Greene was born in New York City, the middle child of five, and grew up in Connecticut. She has worked as a newspaper reporter, an advertising copywriter, and a creative director. She lives in Chapel Hill, North Carolina, with her husband and their son Oliver, an avid fisherman, gardener, inventor, reader, and soccer player. The daughter of acclaimed children's novelist Constance C. Greene, Stephanie Greene makes her children's book debut with *Owen Foote, Second Grade Strongman*.